Dragons Rule,

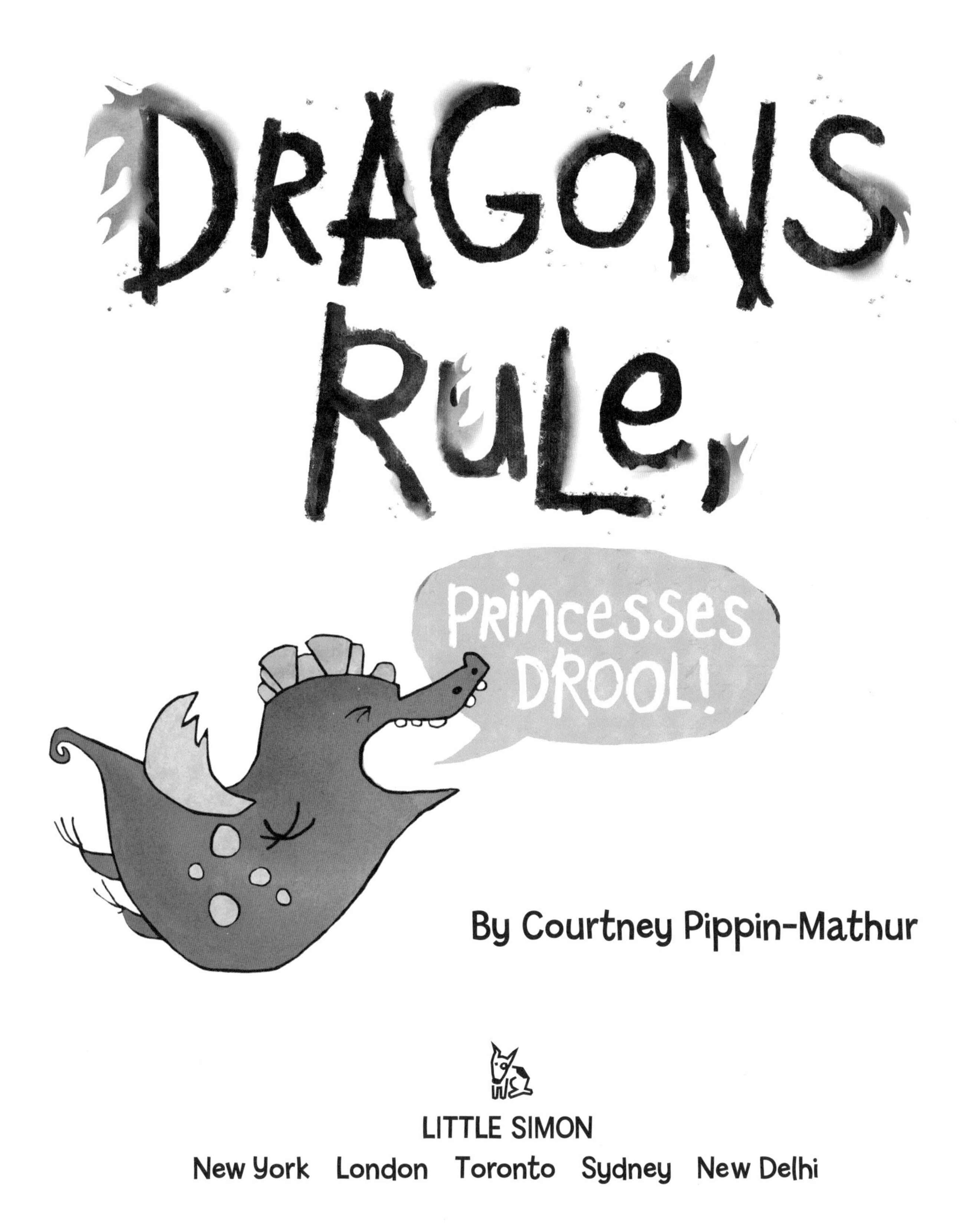

By Courtney Pippin-Mathur

LITTLE SIMON
New York London Toronto Sydney New Delhi

To **Arjun** and **Sachin**,
my favorite dragons

LITTLE SIMON
An imprint of Simon & Schuster Children's Publishing Division
1230 Avenue of the Americas, New York, New York 10020
First Little Simon hardcover edition May 2017

Jacket and interior designed by Chani Yammer and Angela Navarra
Manufactured in China 0217 SCP
10 9 8 7 6 5 4 3 2 1
Cataloging-in-Publication Data is available from the Library of Congress.
ISBN 978-1-4814-6138-2
ISBN 978-1-4814-6139-9 (eBook)

Once there was a Dragon!

He was fierce.
He was strong!

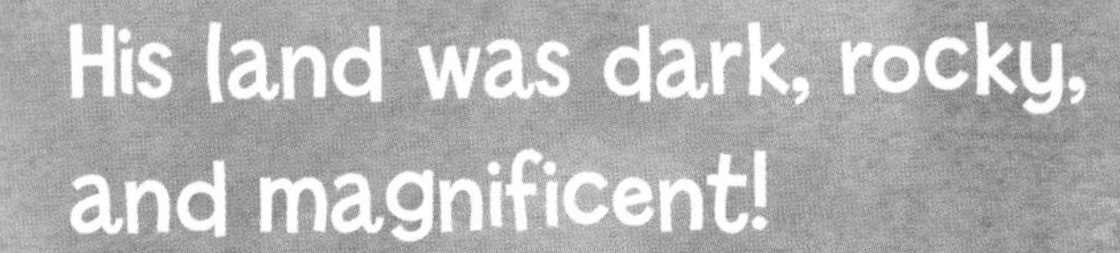

His land was dark, rocky,
and magnificent!

Dragon smoke curled through
the trees, and flames blasted into
the sky, frightening everyone
who came near!

Well, almost everyone.

One day two dangerous creatures
invaded his kingdom.

He did not trust them.

They wore puffy dresses with ruffles.

They pranced.

They even played with the dragons' food.

Still, he tried to teach them the Dragon ways . . .

but they refused to learn.

They were changing the land.

DRAgon PePPER Fields
+ FlowERS

And worse, they were changing his fellow fierce dragons.

Finery had replaced flames.
Cute had replaced ferocious.

The dragon had reached his boiling point!

He must defend his kingdom.
Only he could stop the pastel pests
before it was too late.

There were always knightly creatures searching for adventure and excitement in the dark forest.

Perhaps he would find one to remove the **royal pains.**

So, the dragon invited the knight to rescue the princesses and return them to their castle.

No more pink and puffy!

Ruffles would be banished forever!

But . . .

the knight netted his fellow fierce **dragons instead!**

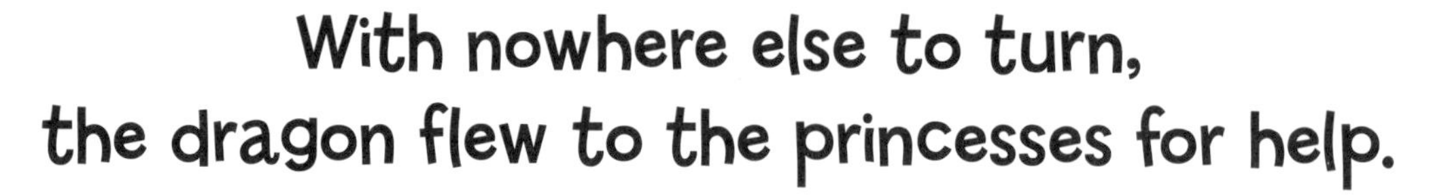
With nowhere else to turn,
the dragon flew to the princesses for help.

They planned.

They snacked.

They sneaked.

Then, softly and delicately,
they let out a . . .

RRRRPP

Now their land is dark, rocky, and colorful! Their flowers curl around the trees and their flames blast into the sky!

They are fierce.
They are strong.

They are FRIENDS!